Life's Recipe for Lemonade

Kamilla "KB" Buckner

DEDICATION

This book is dedicated to my beloved Mother,
Shirley M. Brown

January 31, 1952 – March 18, 2017

Mom, although you are no longer with me
physically, I know you will always be with me in
spirit. Your many sacrifices and unselfish acts of
love not only paved the way for me to become the
woman I am today, but helped to shape the woman I
am. I love and miss you!

CONTENTS

ACKNOWLEDGMENTS

Growing up, I often heard the phrase "It takes a village...." We learned in school that villages are settlements of people clustered around a central point. Well, the central point in the coined phrase, is children. The phrase relied on the sentiments that it takes the cohesiveness and collaborated efforts of a cluster of people to raise a child.

As adults, we no longer require parental rearing, but we do; however, still require proper types of disciplines. In essence, we still need a village, a trusted circle of people, or a team if you will, providing sound wisdom and judgement and holding us accountable to truth and discipline.

My Village

Nathan: You are my biggest supporter! You bring so much joy to my life, I appreciate your wisdom young man. I love you more than the stars buddy!

Brother: I'm finally doing what you asked, "letting my talent shine to give others light & vision!" I love you!

Johnny: You are a rock and that alone speaks volumes. Thank you, my friend!

Roberta: Over 30 years of learning and growing together – true friendship!

Pastor Battle: Sometimes, less is more. You gave me the most important advice to jumpstart me!

To the rest of my family, you guys are the best and I am extremely grateful for you all.

Special Acknowledgment:

Sean: Love covers a multitude of wrongs; you will always be in my heart. I love you brother!

PROLOGUE

The storms of life come in various fashions; but unlike fashion, we don't get to choose which storm to go through on any given day of the week. The unexpected curve balls, coupled with bad decisions, are the brewing of a perfect storm. Life has a way of grabbing hold of you like a bear, squeezing out every ounce of hope, leaving you in a state of brokenness and defeat. I've ridden a many rollercoaster of trials over the years; with no way off as it often appeared, but the worse of them was my addiction. While this book lays no claim to freedom from addictions, it will provide a foundation for a breakthrough; however, the work is up to you.

≈1≈
THE CALM BEFORE THE STORM

The Addictive Personality

As a child, you think and act as such with no thought of repercussions for your actions. I was introduced to an insidious addiction at an early age, gambling. It was fun, exciting, and a quick way to earn a little change to add to my piggy bank – no harm, no foul, right? Couldn't be further away from the side of right. What began as an innocent gesture of fun would eventually pave the way to years of financial and emotional ruin. No one had a prophetic word [or if they did, it was quiet as kept] that I had or would develop an "additive personality."

An additive personality, as I like to define it, is any obsession causing one to escape from the world of reality into a world of temporary pleasure, relinquishing control to make rational decisions. Bottom line, a clear and present pathway to destruction. "The Addiction Center" defined an addictive personality as a "personality that is more likely to become addicted to something. This can include someone becoming extremely passionate about something and developing an obsession or fixation."

An additive personality generally drives people from one addiction to another. In short, they will put down one only to pick up another; and according to "Mayo Clinic Health System," addictive personality traits are associated with anxiety, depression, impulsivity and risk taking. Well, ring the bell four times because I had them all! The most debilitating of them were the anxiety and depression, which I masked very well – "just put on your happy face," I would tell myself and all will be well and there you have it, the calm before the storm!

The more I was around gambling, the more fixated I became; and once I was in, it was all or nothing, it had become my crutch. As an adult, gambling had now become the biggest; well, one of the biggest lies I told myself and others. You see, I was convinced that my financial woes were due to "lack," lack of income (socioeconomic status), lack of support as a single mom, and the "lack" list went on like a criminal rap sheet until I turned into the "Woe, it's me," person. You know those people, they are the ones you quickly turn the corner and run when you see them coming; yea, I'm sure in my insurmountable woes, I caused many to sprint.

To live in a lie is equivalent to living in an escape room in the dark, with no clues or light to guide you to the exit. It didn't help being surrounded by enablers who bought into my lies, those who thought they could "judge" me back to reality, and those who simply said, "she's an adult," neither was the solution – what I needed was someone to love me to truth and accountability while holding me accountable. My addiction, coupled with the caught-off guard curve balls of life; bad relationships, death of loved ones, and inner turmoil, turned into a boulder marked "destruction" rapidly spiraling down the mountain with me as its target! I was broken, ashamed, embarrassed and confused – how could such an intelligent, persevering, person be in such an unequivocal state of despair? I had lost control, boundaries were no longer a factor, I had crossed my own and others. I craved more – it was the peace to a chaotic world, and I needed more because despite the negative impacts and outcomes, I just couldn't stop! I had now entered into what I call the "Bitter Process."

Moment of Reflection

What lie(s) are you living?

_____
_____
_____
_____
_____
_____
_____
_____
_____
_____
_____
_____

Who or what caused you to be in this state?

_____
_____
_____
_____
_____
_____
_____
_____
_____
_____

Have you reestablished boundaries for yourself and others?

_____
_____
_____
_____

_____

_____

_____

_____

_____

_____

_____

_____

_____

What words have you taken ownership of that doesn't belong to you? Someone may have told you that you would never amount to or you're not good at anything – don't take on the ownership of negativity or lies!

_____

_____

_____

_____

_____

_____

_____

_____

_____

_____

_____

Hebrews 10:35-36: [35]Therefore do not throw away your confidence, which has a great reward. [36]For you have need of endurance, so that when you have done the will of God you may receive what is promised.

≈2≈
THE BITTER PROCESS

Lemons add value

We've all heard the adage cliché "When life hands you lemons, make lemonade." Just as the taste of a lemon can be bittersweet, so can the trials of life. However, when challenged, we tend to focus on the bitter rather than the sweet. Truth be told, the only way to the sweet, is through the bitter. The dichotomy is, we don't always taste the sweetness when faced with challenges; be it tragedy, poor decisions, bad relationships, or a Murphy's Law-type situation, "Anything that can go wrong, will go wrong."

To my surprise, I have found that the oblong shaped, bright, yellow-colored fruit that can tighten a face and transform beauty to the look of a beast in a nanosecond, has many added values. Not only is a lemon symbolic of bitterness, but it also symbolizes purification, longevity and love. Lemons are used to detox, cure colds, help with digestive issues and is used for a host of other home remedies. However, lemons like humans, have a transition process and one of the biggest challenges of a lemon tree is, blossom often drop and newly forming fruit fall before it has a chance to grow. All things life will face challenges, it's inevitable, it's part of the growth process.

The Enemy

The enemy of the lemon tree are eight-legged arthropods called citrus mites. They suck the juice from leaves and new growth, ultimately wreaking havoc on the production of quality fruit. Here's some food for thought, "gardeningknowhow" says, "Strong trees can withstand small infestations of mites with little ill effect. The mites are so small that you often cannot see them until damage is severe." I was a strong tree for quite some time, and unable to see the infestation of mites until the damage was done. Other common factors affecting the growth production of a lemon tree are direct sunlight (exposure) and the age of the tree - aye, maturity.

Let's talk about exposure and maturity for a moment. One of my favorite past times is prayer and meditation; particularly, in the morning, it helps to start my day in an appointed direction when my mind is renewed, and I can clearly hear God's guidance. Recently, during my morning meditation, I had an "aha" moment, a moment of revelation; I had begun to understand that exposure is not only an uncovering of something, but it is also a call to action – Wow! That's good stuff right there (as my Pastor would say)! You see, direct sunlight uncovers the fruit that is being produced and calls the tree to action – yep, you guessed it, PRODUCTION! But wait, there's more! This is about to bless you 'real' good as the ole church folks used to say. Ready? Here it goes, "you can't have meaningful production or growth without maturity – BAM! Now, pick your bottom lip up, I warned you.

I can recall numerous times along my journey when I found myself in situations (jobs, friendships, and personal relationships) where it was all so sweet going in, but bitter to its heightened essence coming out - it took me years to learn as inviting as water appears, it only takes a second to jump in, but it may take what seems like an eternity to get out if you don't know how to swim. I dove headfirst into the ocean of gambling. The addiction was also the mite in my life halting production and damaging my fruits – my self-awareness, gifts and talents. Everything and everyone else were to blame for all that was crumbling before my eyes. I didn't have the wherewithal to cope and two of the most important tools in my toolbox were missing; "direct sunlight and maturity." I often gave thought to suicide convincing myself that ending my life would make life better for both my son and me. He would no longer have to worry, and I would no longer cause him or myself anymore pain. Oh, the power of dysfunctional thoughts!

Almost there

The bitter process of our lives is always the toughest pill to swallow. You haven't quite reached the stage of maturity just yet, but you are getting ready to be exposed to the dawn of a new day; however, I must warn you, it's not going to be easy. When that direct sunlight hits, it's going to burn like a hot summer's day in the middle of August with an unbearable heat index where the temperature may read 80 degrees, but it feels like 110. It's going to be ok to not be "okay," but you have to keep pushing! Also, during this process, we tend to neutralize - meaning we're quick to add a little flavor by hiding, overcompensating and self-medicating (to achieve that feeling of reward the brain so desperately seeks, providing a false sense of satisfaction), only to treat the symptoms and not the root cause of the problem. That first ray of light will be so blinding, it will cause you to begin shifting the blame elsewhere because it takes the focus off of you. But when you shift blame, you're actually projecting your inner battle of turmoil onto others who quickly become the brunt of your pain and victimized mentally as you become swallowed up in your own delusion. You know what I'm talking about, the no one understands; everyone's against me-type delusion and confabulation. Or, shall I say, the lies you tell yourself until your eyes adjust to the light and you come to the realization, that all this time, you were the only invitee to the pity party! Maturity is on its way, just a few more stops to go. The first stop is at the corner of dancing to your favorite tune "Woe, It's Me, you need to exit that party immediately leaving behind the wrapped-up party favors of guilt, shame, pity, embarrassment, and condemnation – RUN! There's someone waiting to meet you, a new you, but she won't be revealed just yet, she'll be introduced right after the "Purification Process."

Moment of Reflection

How many times have you dropped off (given up) before the finish (your chance to grow)?

_____

_____

_____

_____

_____

_____

_____

_____

_____

_____

_____

_____

_____

Who or what are the mites in your life damaging your fruit or wreaking havoc on your production or growth?

_____

_____

_____

_____

_____

_____

_____

_____

_____

_____

_____

_____

Ecclesiastes 9:11 I have seen something else under the sun: The race is not to the swift or the battle to the strong, nor does food come to the wise or wealth to the brilliant or favor to the learned; but time and chance happen to them all.

≈3≈
THE PURIFICATION PROCESS

Life Happens

The bitter process was a season of pruning; you made mistakes and the wisdom or lessons learned has taught you to remove the mites preventing healthy growth. The purification process is where the beauty begins to unfold, but not before the final exam. Have you been studying? There will certainly be pop-up quizzes and random tests.

Now that your mite infestation (baggage, people, things, false thoughts, etc.) has been exposed, it's time to cleanse – to free yourself from the burden of guilt. This aids in the preparation of "life happens" moments; it sets you up for the response as you move from being reactive to proactive. Your mental and emotional state is better equipped to handle the pressure without the excess baggage of the bitter process. Unfortunately, for me, it took the passing of my family's matriarch, my beloved mother, for me to finally reach this magical place in my life.

Exactly one month prior to my Mom being diagnosed with cancer, for the first time, I let her into my world of addiction. I will never forget the day, September 22, 2017, to be exact. It was a beautiful Saturday afternoon, Mother had dropped by for a visit, we started out with small talk and banter back and forth when suddenly, my heart erupted, spilling over into diarrhea of the mouth. Mom, I softly whispered as a child about to fearfully confess a mischief and anticipating the worst, "I'm sick." I could see the terror in her eyes as she anxiously braced herself for what would come next. What do you mean, you're sick? She asked. Something is wrong with me I blurted out as the tears followed and my adult body, had in an instance, regressed into a fetal posture. I continued on, "as much as I have tried to stop, I just can't, I need help!" In that moment, no further explanation was warranted, Mom inferred and drew the spot-on conclusion. She replied, "I just had a conversation with my co-worker the other day who explained to me what addiction was like and I immediately thought of you." Her response immediately began to bring my body back to an upright position as I inwardly shouted for joy "finally, she gets me – I'm free! I felt the weight of years' worth of burdens of grief and disappointment drop instantly. I could have been the star in my own Weight Watcher's commercial; "I lost 10 pounds in 30 minutes from a healthy heaping of confession. I feel Gr-e--a-t!

After many failed attempts to overcome this obstacle, I was now on the road to recovery. Mom and I mapped out plans, she held me accountable and my feet to the fire – I was riding the magic carpet to freedom, but as we all know, magic is only an illusion of what we think we see. My magic carpet was violently ripped from underneath me [here comes the pop-up quizzes and tests] when Mom was diagnosed with not one, but two tumors that metastasized in her brain; and four months later my beloved gift was gone. Do I need to tell you what happen next? It was like being involved in a multiple pile-up car accident with me on the bottom of the pile, except I wasn't in a car. I was back at ground zero! I went back and dusted off that old invitation to that pity party; dressed myself up in the finest bitter, anger, and pity clothing I could find while pumping the volume to that old familiar tune, "Woe,

It's Me!" I was partying like a "Rock Star!" Hope you didn't think it would stop there – seven months later, my Dad passed in the same manner as Mom. This can't be happening! God, you are hilarious, I sarcastically thought. Is this some sort of cruel joke? If that weren't enough, adding more salt to the already split wide-opened wounds, my youngest brother, whom I adore, cut all ties with his siblings. All hopes for any resiliency were out the window. I was the modern-day version of Colonel Steve Austin from the 70's television series, "The Six Million Dollar Man." Stand by, be back to connect the dots in a bit.

Picking up the Broken Pieces

I am a fan of Iyanla Vanzant. Ms. Vanzant is an inspirational speaker, life coach, and teacher to name a few; and the television host of "Iyanla, Fix My Life." She is known for encouraging broken people to do the work! I recall one evening leaving work after a long, and stressful day, I was driving down 495 filled with a stream of emotions, in a perilous currant. I needed some reassurance, so I called my eldest brother to no avail, I then reached out to his wife, my best friend; also, to no avail. I hung up and hit the redial again, the same, no response. Where are people when you need them? I shouted! At this point, I just burst into tears and along with the tears ushered in the words, "it's time to do the work!" Alas, a breakthrough, an epiphany, "do the work!" I held on to those words as though I were protecting gold; in essence, I was. The gold was me having been tried, but about to come through as pure gold. Finally, I arrived home with gusto, anxious to break ground on the new renovation – a new me.

Now, back to Colonel Austin, played by Lee Majors, the star of the sci-fi television series. Colonel Austin was an astronaut who suffered a horrific NASA test flight accident leaving him severely injured. What I recall about the opening of the show was the somewhat soft, spoken, confident declaration of Oscar from the Office of Scientific Intelligence (the OSI) stating, "We can rebuild him; better, stronger, faster! Colonel Austin, while science fiction, was hit by life, but his broken pieces were used to make him better – it was a six-million-dollar project hence, the "Six Million Dollar Man." In some respects, I consider my life a project; well, not necessarily a project, but definitely a puzzle – fortunately for me, it didn't cost six-million-dollars to rebuild. However, it did cost a great deal of hard work, sweat, tears, and muscle memory to rebuild what had been torn down.

Maturity Arrives

We all can learn a thing or two from the project of Colonel Austin. One, never discard broken pieces, they hold value; and two, it takes a team to help you rebuild, but it requires wisdom, dedication and maturity.

A lemon tree requires three to five years to reach maturity. Similar to the lemon tree, it takes years of experience, trial and error and let's not forget, a village (your team), people who have your best interest at heart, to hold you up and accountable in order to perfect maturity (Thank God for the bitter and purification process). We, as humans, become so accustomed to doing things on our own that we negate the fact that we were not created to do life alone. When we find ourselves in an isolated state, pain usually ends up being the culprit; and immediately the guards go up and the doors shut (to healthy love and affection). Not the wisest coping mechanism, might I add. Now, don't misunderstand, there are times when we need to get alone and shut out the noise around us in order to declutter and detoxify our mind and soul from the garbage, we feed it, i.e., the news, gossip, cares of the world, etc. However, shutting down too long in response to being hurt will lead to emotional numbness and stonewalling the people you love, escalating the situation you were attempting to avert. This is why maturity must be perfected, it is the phase where not only do you begin to build meaningful and healthy relationships, beginning with yourself, but a phase where you learn to face your pain and process accordingly in a healthy manner for all involved. A destination, I so desperately, needed to reach.

Back to the day of my epiphany, upon my arrival home, I got in a quiet space and I began to reflect and lay out all the pieces to the puzzle – discarding nothing. I sorted the pieces by pattern (repetition), then I connected the patterns with the triggers (cause and effect). Next, I began to work on the corners (the lies I held on to in the corners of my mind); and finally, I worked the center (the heart and soul) – I had to do some serious soul-searching and it wasn't pretty, some hideous stuff came out of that closet – thank God for my village, counselors and people with strong backbones who put up with me. This process of rebuilding was under construction for four years; it was slowed down a time or two from setbacks and hurdles, but by God's mercy and grace, I kept pushing; the more I pushed, the stronger I became (muscle memory). My spiritual vision was sharpened, and wisdom sought after me knocking down my door – the one door I am finally glad to have opened, maturity had arrived!

Your past has not come full circle to its complete redemption until you allow Christ to not only defuse it, but also to use it.

-Beth Moore

Moment of Reflection

Who or what is knocking at your door (enticing you)?

_____

_____

_____

_____

_____

_____

_____

_____

_____

_____

_____

_____

What doors do you need to close?

_____

_____

_____

_____

_____

_____

_____

_____

_____

_____

_____

_____

What do you need to make room for?

_____

_____

_____

_____

_____

_____

_____

_____

_____

_____

_____

_____

Proverbs 1:10 My son, if sinful men entice you, do not give in to them. Revelation 3:7 These are the words of him who is holy and true, who holds the key of David. What he opens no one can shut, and what he shuts no one can open.

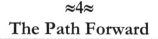

The Path Forward

The Big Reveal

I must say, of the two transitional phases, the Purifying Process was the hardest for me. It forced me to see who I was at the time, a person, whom not only did I not love, but I didn't like as well. I was a woman on the run, cutting every corner to avoid my pain, but I have no regrets and I am eternally grateful to my Lord who specializes in multiple do-overs and second chances. His patience, guidance and love for me gave me the strength to persevere; and allowed me to see my true worth. With that, I was able to forgive myself and blossom into a woman whom I now adore! I am addiction free and the most joyous I've ever been – I can look in the mirror now with recognition of the person who is staring back, the renovation is complete! The mites that damaged my lemons and hindered my growth no longer exist. I am ripening now, and my color has changed, no longer blemished, my beautiful fruit is being produced! I've learned to embrace and love myself; watch the beauty of it spill over into my relationships and pour back into me.

Love, Wisdom, Pain

There are so many definitions of the four-lettered word "love," but the one that holds the most value to me comes from the Greek word "agape." I can sum it up in two words: unconditional and selfless. First, let me dispel the myth that it doesn't cost anything to love, it does, there's a price to pay for everything. But, to love unconditionally speaks volumes to the person who extends it. It says I am willing to forgive myself and others; I am disciplined and mature enough to know when to let go of hurt and how to healthily respond; I have the wisdom to know when and what to change; I am not responsible for changing others; I recognize that I have to lay down my life (old ways) to pick it up again (new beginning); and I value my worth because I see myself just as I was created, fearfully and wonderfully made.

In my limited observations, I have heard some say being "selfless" is a form of weakness, I beg to differ. Being weak, my friend, is having a talent; hogging it or being too intimidated by fear to use it. However, to be selfless, if I may define and defend, is to recognize that you are not the center of everything life. Yes, you matter, and you are extremely important; however, you were created for purpose (in the plural sense), which means your life has meaning for others as well, and it takes love, strength and endurance to deny yourself (humility) to fulfill the purpose.

The Wisdom of Pain

Oh, pain, what is thy purpose?
What do you gain from my suffering?
You are strong and powerful bringing
the strongest man to his knees.

Oh, pain, what is thy purpose?
Will you flee from me please!
What is it you desire of me when awakened from my sleep?
What is it you desire of me when I am unable to sleep?

Is it your goal to rob me of my joy and keep me off my feet?
Oh, pain, what is thy purpose, what do you seek?

Beloved, don't be dismayed.
I've come to motivate you and make you aware.
To perfect your strength in moments of despair.

It is I who reveals your strength when no one else cares.
I am the stimuli to your faith and your opportunity to victory.

It is I who gives ear to your body's plea when it cries out, why
have you neglected me?
I am the key to your inner strength.
I give you push back when you feel you can't go on.
It is I who leads you to an assignment that you otherwise would
have let undone.

So beloved, don't be so quick to rid yourself of me.
Though I may sting for a brief moment in time,
You will come to understand my true purpose when your focus
is truly aligned.

≈5≈

The Power of Faith and Affirmations

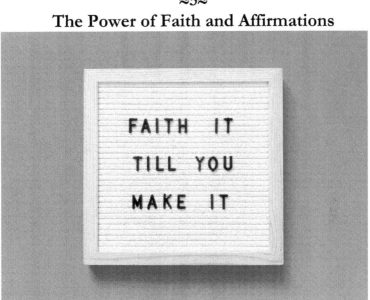

Kicking your Faith into Action

We, all, have a built-in longing to be accepted and I would dare say that many have a self-imposed slavery to fear of how they are viewed by others. This type of fear can lead to emotionally driven impulsive behaviors in an attempt to gain sought-after approval. Along my healing journey, I had obtained a confidence and approval I'd never experience before. I had reassurance from the Lord that all things would work together for my good according to his purpose (Rom. 8:28); I know the plans I have for you, declares the Lord, plans to prosper you and not to harm you, plans to give you hope and a future (Jeremiah 29:11); and Those who place their trust in the Lord will never be put to shame (Psalm 25:1). These were holy scriptures I was all too familiar with but having knowledge without action is meaningless and renders the knowledge powerless. It wasn't until my faith aligned with those words (his promises), I stopped consuming my myself with what I perceived others to think of me, learned to deny my flesh through fasting, and embrace my pain, that I was able to grab the bull by the horn and take charge confidently knowing that whatever is intended to harm me, will all work out for my good. I felt like Linus (from Charlie Brown), these words will forever be my security blanket travelling with me (in my heart) wither I go. One must fall in order to rise; and it's in the valley (the fall) where the lessons are learned to elevate you, if, you allow wisdom to be your teacher!

Disclaimer: Faith doesn't prevent trials but reassures one that God is in control in the midst of aversity.

Moment of Reflection

What are you affirming over your life?

_____

_____

_____

_____

_____

_____

_____

_____

_____

_____

_____

_____

_____

What can you change in your life, your community, by turning knowledge into action?

_____

_____

_____

_____

_____

_____

_____

_____

_____

_____

_____

_____

Proverbs 18:21 The tongue has power of life and death, and those who love it will eat its fruit.

It's Time to do the Work

In the Bitter Process, you learned how your enemy (baggage) can alter or stop your production. You also learned in the Purification Process the importance of maturity. Now, it's time to put the tools in action. In a separate journal, write your responses to the "Moments of Reflections," re-read the Poem "The Wisdom of Pain." Compare and contrast your responses to the Poem, identify your assignment, make your declaration, go forth and conquer, but not before you make that lemonade:

Declaration

_____ (months or year) from now, I will be better spiritually, physically, mentally, and financially. I will no longer allow _____ to pull me down or plant seeds of lies, confusion or negativity in my soil. From this moment forward, I will produce ripe, bright-colored fruit and I choose to view my pain and the pain of others through the eyes of wisdom!

Now about that Lemonade

As with all trees and flowers, it takes the planting of seeds with the right amount of soil, which is why you should never be ashamed of the dirt in your life because it's what blossoms in the end that matters. Eventually, the seeds become roots, the roots become vines, the vines become branches and the branches leaves; and in this case, the leaves become fruit – at the ripening time, ready to be plucked. Get ready to be plucked for that tall, thirst-quenching glass of lemonade. Now, you are ready to quench the thirst of others (your pain has become your ministry).

The recipe:
1. Gather as many lemons (life's lessons and experiences) as you can.
2. Squeeze all the bitter juice (pain) from each lemon.
3. Add as much water (purification) as needed.
4. Stir in the sweet savory taste of love in abundance.
5. Be sure to gently mix all of the ingredients together and be ready to pour, for pretty soon, you will be a tree firmly planted by the rivers; serving all who thirst.
6. More importantly, don't forget to top it off with a little faith.

≈6≈
Concluding Reflections

Experience + Endurance = Hope

If you have ever attempted to put together a one-thousand-piece puzzle, you are aware of how challenging the experience can be. It may take hours, days, or even months to connect the interrelated parts, but it is the endurance that offers the ray of hope to arrive at the finished product, the picture on the outside of the box.

You are the beautiful image on the outside of the box. Every trial in your life plays an intricate role in your development – knowing that tribulation worketh patience; and patience, experience; and experience, hope (Rom. 5:3-4).

Help is on the way

If you or someone you know is struggling with an addiction, I strongly encourage you to use every resource available to conquer the addiction and take back your control. Be transparent and seek wise counseling and remember:

1. You're only as accurate as your awareness: Stay vigilant, sober and self-aware.
2. You're only as sick as your secrets: Reveal, confront, heal.
3. You're only as confident as you believe: Be bold, conquer, achieve.

By The Recovery Village
Editor Camille Renzoni
Medically Reviewed By Eric Patterson, LPC
Updated on 01/20/20

7 Types of Gamblers: Which One Are You?

Although all addictions have the power to create havoc in a person's life, not all addictions are the same, and not all people experience addiction in the same way.

A person with an opioid use disorder, for example, could either be abusing medications prescribed by their doctor or abusing heroin from the street. Their situations and experiences are completely different.

The same is true with gamblers and people who struggle with gambling addiction. Gamblers show addictive behaviors in various ways. To understand and treat the problem, it's necessary to understand the type of addiction and the individual's unique situation. In answer to the frequently searched question, "Which type of gambler am I?" This overview of seven types of gamblers can be helpful.

1. Professional Gamblers

Professional gamblers are a rarity. People who gamble professionally make a living by gambling. Somehow, they confront systems that are built around taking their money and come out ahead.

Being a professional gambler takes an extraordinary level of:

Patience
Frustration tolerance
Intelligence
Self-control

Successful professional gamblers continually weigh the odds of each situation to decide how to proceed. Impulsivity and anger stand in the way of their performance, so professionals dismiss these traits.

It is important to note that professional gamblers will not usually be addicted to the act of gambling. Addictions can diminish self-control and rational thinking, which would undoubtedly cause more losses than wins.

2. Casual Social Gamblers

A casual, social gambler is much more common than a professional player. A casual gambler may stop in a casino from time to time, spending a moderate amount of money on slots or blackjack and then head home at the end of the night. They might also join friends for a fantasy football league or Friday night poker game.

For the casual, social gambler, the act is not about the strong desire to win. This type of gambler is interested in spending time with friends, meeting new people and engaging in some rest and relaxation to relieve stress.

The casual, social gambler is comparable to a social drinker. A social drinker may head to the bar after work some days, but the experience is more about socializing with similar people to de-stress. Alcohol, or gambling, in this case, is not the primary focus.

3. Serious Social Gamblers

Gambling can be either a positive or a negative coping skill. The casual gambler uses gambling as one of their various available outlets, but the serious social gambler relies solely on gambling to cope.

While negative coping skills seem useful in the moment, they only lead to problems in the future. With long hours spent gambling to cope with stress, serious social gamblers may begin sliding toward problematic gambling while struggling to maintain family obligations, work and friendships.

4. Relief and Escape Gamblers

The National Institute on Drug Abuse reports that addictions commonly form when people engage in behaviors, like using drugs or gambling, to fulfill an emotional need. Relief and escape gamblers may only seek out gambling as a way to manage their depression, anxiety or other causes of stress.

Escape gamblers may be pretty unsuccessful at winning, though. Due to their emotional state, their decision making and judgment can be poor. Relief and escape gamblers could lose huge amounts of money in a short amount of time and feel higher stress, anxiety and depression in the long-term.

Relief and escape gamblers benefit from expanded coping skills to address their emotional needs.

5. Conservative Gamblers

Rather than seeking the thrill of winning or the social aspect of gambling, conservative gamblers are interested in the experience. They want to try playing slots or rolling the dice because they have seen the games on television or in movies and are curious.

Conservative gamblers likely place a modest budget or time limit on their gambling and stick to it whether they win or lose. This practice makes problematic or addictive gambling very rare among conservative gamblers.

6. Personality Gamblers

For better or worse, the above gambler types all involve activity that is legal, even if it could become problematic. The personality gamblers — sometimes called antisocial gamblers — are different because they behave in illegal ways.

These gamblers want to make large amounts of money gambling by any means necessary. Personality gamblers may lie, cheat, steal and deceive other players or people in charge to come out on top. Their tactics could be simple like hiding a card up their sleeve, or elaborate, like conspiring to fix a race or sporting event.

For the personality gambler, gambling is an issue, but there could be other facets of their criminal activity and mental health that need equal attention from professionals.

7. Compulsive Gamblers

Compulsive gamblers lead lives that are entirely controlled by gambling and money. Even though they might not want to admit it, they frequently display signs of a gambling disorder like:

Spending too much time gambling
Making unsuccessful attempts to cut back or stop gambling
Continuing to gamble despite issues with relationships, work, school or home life caused by gambling
Constantly chasing the next win to compensate for the last loss
Compulsive gamblers typically need professional treatment and support from their loved ones to avoid worsening life circumstances. Compulsive gambling can quickly consume a person's life.

Notes

Dedication

1. *https://elements.envato.com/photos/lighthouse/pg-3*

The Calm Before the Storm

1. *https://elements.envato.com/photos/the+calm+before+the+storm*
2. *www.addictioncenter.com*
3. *www.mayoclinic.org*

The Bitter Process

1. *www.saje.com*
2. *www.gardeningknowhow.com*
3. *https://elements.envato.com/photos/bitter/pg-2*

The Purification Process

1. *Beth Moore, So Long Insecurity (Carol Stream, IL: Tyndale, 2010), 311.*

The Power of Faith and Affirmations

1. *https://elements.envato.com/faith-FZNRTLR*
2. *https://elements.envato.com/photos/lemon+and+mint*

7 Types of Gamblers: Which One are You?

1. *https://www.therecoveryvillage.com/process-addiction/compulsive-gambling/related/types-of-gamblers/*

ABOUT THE AUTHOR

Kamilla Buckner's passion is to serve others in love leading them to knowledge, understanding and wisdom. She believes in community and is a community activist. Kamilla's messages come from the heart and is driven by the inspired Word of God; woven with personal life experiences and practical truths. She is also a blogger, blogging about her passions from injustices to peace, and poetry.

Kamilla lives in Maryland with her family. She serves as an intercessory prayer on behalf of others in her church and community. She enjoys studying and teaching the Holy Bible and participating in weekly prayer calls.

Outside of writing, Kamilla's favorite hobby is shooting a great game of pool.

To connect with more of Kamilla's writings, visit her website at:

www.thecornertruth.com

Made in the USA
Middletown, DE
15 September 2022

10452490R00022